Syllabus

IN THE PHILOSOPHY OF EDUCATION

Questions for Discussion With Reading References and Topics for Papers

MAXWELL PRESS

Syllabus

IN THE PHILOSOPHY OF EDUCATION

Questions for Discussion With Reading References and Topics for Papers

WILLIAM HEARD KILPATRICK

Professor of Education, Teachers College

MAXWELL PRESS

Chennai   New Delhi

MAXWELL PRESS

An Imprint of MJP Publishers

ISBN 978-93-5528-170-8 **MAXWELL PRESS**

All rights reserved
Printed and bound in India

No. 44, Nallathambi Street,
Triplicane,
Chennai 600 005

MJP 1412 © Publishers, 2022

Publisher : **C. Janarthanan**

PUBLISHER'S NOTE

The legacy of a country is in its varied cultural heritage, historical literature, developments in the field of economy and science. The top nations in the world are competing in the field of science, economy and literature. This vast legacy has to be conserved and documented so that it can be bestowed to the future generation. The knowledge of this legacy is slowly getting perished in the present generation due to lack of documentation.

Keeping this in mind, the concern with retrospective acquiring of rare books has been accented recently by the burgeoning reprint industry. MAXWELL PRESS is gratified to retrieve the rare collections with a view to bring back those books that were landmarks in their time.

In this effort, a series of rare books would be republished under the banner, "MAXWELL PRESS". The books in the reprint series have been carefully selected for their contemporary usefulness as well as their historical importance within the intellectual. We reconstruct the book with slight enhancements made for better presentation, without affecting the contents of the original edition.

Most of the works selected for republishing covers a huge range of subjects, from history to anthropology. We believe this reprint edition will be a service to the numerous researchers and practitioners active in this fascinating field. We allow readers to experience the wonder of peering into a scholarly work of the highest order and seminal significance.

MAXWELL PRESS

INTRODUCTORY STATEMENT

THE topics and questions herein presented have grown up in the actual class-room experience of the past ten years. Until 1921 the questions were given to the class, topic at a time, on separate sheets, and each succeeding year underwent more or less modification. To retain the advantage of constant revision each printed edition is limited to enough copies to last for just one year.

The daily work of the classes where these questions are used consists of three parts: (1) individual reading and study of the topic; (2) a preliminary consideration of the questions in a voluntary "discussion group" of from five to ten class members; finally (3) the discussion of the questions in class by the students under the direction of the instructor. The procedure is designed to make the students think for themselves, to avoid giving to them ready-made opinions. The effort is to bring home to each student some of the more vital problems in the philosophy of education. In the class discussion each student is expected to be able and ready to present and maintain an intelligent position on each question. Opposing considerations are contrasted and discussed. All this to the end that the student may feel the grip of the problem under consideration and obtain at least a fair idea of the contending principles at issue. That the students may more certainly do their own thinking and more freely present their views, the instructor's view is reserved for the final summing up, and then if given is presented merely as a personal opinion which the students may be interested to hear.

The bibliographical references are for daily use and make no pretense at completeness. Rather do they refer to books available for the class in the Teachers College library. Possibly later editions of this pamphlet may remedy some deficiencies along this line. The Source Quotations found in the reading lists refer to a manuscript collection of pertinent sources on file in the Teachers College library. Perhaps at some later day these may appear in book form. The source quotations assigned to any topic are divided generally into sets (separated by semicolons) according as they group themselves by common pertinence to the several subordinate aspects of the topic under consideration. Those especially important are starred. The order of the other items in each reading list is determined mainly by relative pertinence to the topic under consideration but partly from their practical availability in the library. Those ranking highest are put first.

TABLE OF CONTENTS

REFERENCE BOOKS

Abbott, Lyman. *The Spirit of Democracy*. Houghton Mifflin 1910.
Addams, Jane. *Democracy and Social Ethics*. Macmillan 1902.
Alexander, Thomas. *Prussian Elementary Schools*. Macmillan 1918.
Angell, J. R. *Psychology*. Holt 1908.
Bachman, F. P. *Principles of Elementary Education*. Heath 1915.
Bagehot, Walter. *Physics and Politics*. Appleton 1887.
Bagley, W. C. *Educative Process*. Macmillan 1905.
Bagley, W. C. *Educational Values*. Macmillan 1911.
Bagley, W. C. *School Discipline*. Macmillan 1914.
Baldwin, J. M. *Dictionary of Philosophy and Psychology*. Macmillan 1920.
Baldwin, J. M. *Individual and Society*. Badger 1911.
Baldwin, J. M. *Social and Ethical Interpretation*. Macmillan 1906.
Barker, Ernest. *Political Thought in England: from Herbert Spencer to the Present Day*. Holt 1915.
Berkson, I. B. *Theories of Americanization*. Teachers College 1920.
Betts, G. H. *Classroom Methods and Management*. Bobbs Merrill 1917.
Betts, G. H. *Social Principles of Education*. Scribner 1912.
Blackmar, F. W. and Gillin, J. L. *Outlines of Sociology*. Macmillan 1905.
Bobbitt, J. F. *The Curriculum*. Houghton Mifflin 1918.
Bonser, F. G. *Elementary School Curriculum*. Macmillan 1920.
Bradley, F. H. *Ethical Studies*. Stechert 1904.
Branom, M. E. *Project Method in Education*. Badger 1919.
Breese, B. B. *Psychology*. Scribner 1917.
Brown, W. Jethro. *The Underlying Principles of Modern Legislation*. Dutton 1915.
Bryce, James. *American Commonwealth*. 2 vols. Macmillan, new edition, 1915. Abridged edition, 1909.
Bryce, James. *Modern Democracies*. 2 vols. Macmillan 1921.
Burgess, E. W. *Function of Socialization in Social Evolution*. University of Chicago Press 1916.
Bury, J. H. *History of Freedom of Thought*. Williams and Norgate, London 1913.
Butler, N. M. *Meaning of Education*. Scribner 1915.
Butler, N. M. *True and False Democracy*. Scribner 1907.
Canby, H. S. *Education by Violence*. Macmillan 1919.
Carver, Thomas N. *Principles of Political Economy*. Ginn 1919.
Catholic Encyclopedia. Encyclopedia Press 1907–14.
Chafee, Zechariah, Jr., *Freedom of Speech*. Harcourt, Brace and Howe 1920.
Charters, W. W. *Methods of Teaching*. Row Peterson 1912.
Charters, W. W. *Teaching the Common Branches*. Houghton Mifflin 1917.
Coe, G. A. *Psychology of Religion*. University of Chicago Press 1916.
Coe, G. A. *Social Theory of Religious Education*. Scribner 1917.
Coffin, J. H. *Socialized Conscience*. Warwick and York 1913.

Colvin, S. S. *Learning Process*. Macmillan 1911.
Colvin, S. S. and Bagley, W. C *Human Behavior*. Macmillan 1913.
Conklin, E. G. *Heredity and Environment in the Development of Men*. Princeton University Press. 1st edition 1914. 3rd edition 1920.
Conn, H. W. *Social Heredity and Social Evolution*. Abingdon Press 1914.
Cook, Caldwell. *The Play Way*. F. A. Stokes 1917.
Cooley, C. H. *Human Nature and the Social Order*. Scribner 1902.
Cooley, C. H. *Social Organization*. Scribner 1909.
Cooley, C. H. *Social Process*. Scribner 1918.
Croly, H. *The Promise of American Life*. Macmillan 1912.
Cubberley, E. P. *Changing Conceptions in Education*. Houghton Mifflin 1909.
Cubberley, E. P. *School Funds and Their Apportionment*. Teachers College 1905.
Cubberley, E. P. *Public School Administration*. Houghton Mifflin 1916.
Cubberley, E. P. *Readings in the History of Education*. Houghton Mifflin 1920.
Cubberley, E. P. and Elliott, E. C. *Source Book—State and County School Administration*. Macmillan 1915.
Dealey, J. Q. *Sociology*. Silver Burdett 1909.
Dewey, John. *Child and Curriculum*. University of Chicago Press 1902.
Dewey, John. *Democracy and Education*. Macmillan 1916.
Dewey, John. *Educational Situation*. University of Chicago Press 1902.
Dewey, John. *How We Think*. Heath 1910.
Dewey, John. *Interest and Effort in Education*. Houghton Mifflin 1913.
Dewey, John. *Moral Principles in Education*. Houghton Mifflin 1909.
Dewey, John. *My Pedagogic Creed*. Flanagan 1910.
Dewey, John. *School and Society*. University of Chicago Press 1915.
Dewey, John. *Schools of Tomorrow*. Dutton 1915.
Dewey and Tufts. *Ethics*. Holt 1908.
Dole, C. F. *The American Citizen*. Heath 1891.
Dole, C. F. *Ethics of Progress*. Crowell 1909.
Draper, S. S. *American Education*. Houghton Mifflin 1909.
Drever, James. *Instincts in Man*. Cambridge (Eng.) University Press 1917.
Dunney, Joseph A. *The Parish School*. Macmillan 1921.
Dutton, S. and Snedden, D. *Administration of Public Education in the United States*. Macmillan 1912.
Earhart, Lida B. *Types of Teaching*. Houghton Mifflin 1915.
Eliot, C. W. *American Contributions to Civilization*. Century 1909.
Eliot, C. W. *Educational Reform*. Century 1905.
Ellwood, C. A. *Introduction to Social Psychology*. Appleton 1917.
Ellwood, C. A. *The Social Problem*. Macmillan 1915.
Ellwood, C. A. *Sociology and Modern Social Problems*. American Book 1913
Ellwood, C. A. *Sociology in Its Psychological Aspects*. Appleton 1912.
Faguet, Emile. *The Cult of Incompetence*. Dutton 1916.
Fairbanks, Arthur. *Introduction to Sociology*. Scribner 1896.
Farrington, F. E. *French Secondary Schools*. Longmans 1915.
Fite, Warner. *Individualism*. Longmans 1911.
Fite, Warner. *Introductory Study of Ethics*. Longmans 1903.
Giddings, F. H. *Democracy and Empire*. Macmillan 1900.

Giddings, F. H. *Elements of Sociology.* Macmillan 1898.

Giddings, F. H. *Principles of Sociology.* Macmillan 1896.

Giddings, F. H. *Studies in the Theory of Human Society.* Macmillan 1922.

Giddings, F. H. *Theory of Socialization.* Macmillan 1897.

Gillette, J. M. *Vocational Education.* American Book 1910.

Goddard, H. H. *Human Efficiency and Levels of Intelligence.* Princeton University Press 1920.

Hadley, A. T. *Education of the American Citizen.* Yale University Press 1912.

Hadley, A. T. *Relations between Freedom and Responsibility in the Evolution of Democratic Government.* Yale University Press 1903.

Hanus, P. H. *Educational Aims and Educational Values.* Macmillan 1899.

Hastings, James. *Encyclopedia of Religion and Ethics.* 12 vols. Scribner 1908–1922.

Hayes, E. C. *Introduction to the Study of Sociology.* Appleton 1915.

Henderson, E. N. *Textbook in Principles of Education.* Macmillan 1910.

Hobhouse, L. T. *Liberalism.* Holt 1911.

Hobhouse, L. T. *Social Evolution and Political Theory.* Columbia University Press 1911.

Horne, H. H. *Philosophy of Education.* Macmillan 1904.

Howe, F. C. *Socialized Germany.* Scribner 1915.

Huntington, Ellsworth and Cushing, S. W. *Principles of Human Geography.* Wiley 1921.

Inglis, Alexander. *Principles of Secondary Education.* Houghton Mifflin 1918.

James, William. *Principles of Psychology.* 2 vols. Holt 1890.

James, William. *Psychology, Brief Course.* Holt 1892.

James, William. *Some Problems of Philosophy.* Longmans 1911.

James, William. *Talks to Teachers on Psychology.* Holt 1899.

Jordan, David S. *Footnotes to Evolution.* Appleton 1898.

Kilpatrick, W. H. *The Project Method.* Teachers College 1918.

Kirkpatrick, E. A. *Fundamentals of Child Study.* Macmillan 1917.

Kirkpatrick, E. A. *The Individual in the Making.* Houghton Mifflin 1911.

Lippmann, Walter. *Public Opinion.* Harcourt, Brace and Howe. 1921.

Lowell, A. L. *Public Opinion and Popular Government.* Longmans 1914.

Lowie, R. H. *Primitive Society.* Boni and Liveright 1920.

Lull, H. G. *Project Method of Learning.* Kansas State Normal School (Emporia) 1920

Lull, H. G. and Wilson, H. B. *Redirection of High School Instruction.* Lippincott 1921.

MacCunn, John. *The Making of Character.* Macmillan 1913.

MacDougall, William. *Introduction to Social Psychology.* J. W. Luce 1918.

Maciver, R. M. *Community: A Sociological Study.* Macmillan 1917.

McKechnie, W. S. *The State and the Individual.* MacLehose, Glasgow, 1896.

Mackenzie, J. S. *Manual of Ethics.* Hinds 1901.

McMurry, F. M. *Elementary School Standards.* World Book 1913.

McMurry, F. M. *How to Study.* Houghton Mifflin 1909.

MacVannel, J. A. *Outlines of a Course in Philosophy of Education.* Macmillan 1912.

Marot, Helen. *Creative Impulse in Industry.* Dutton 1918.

Massachusetts Commission on Immigration Report. Wright and Potter Printing Co., Boston, 1914.

Mezes, S. E. *Ethics.* Macmillan 1901.

Mill, J. S. *Liberty.* Longmans 1913.

Miller, Irving E. *Education for the Needs of Life.* Macmillan 1917.

Monroe, Paul. *Cyclopedia of Education.* Macmillan 1911–13.

Monroe, Paul. *History of Education.* Macmillan 1905.

Moore, E. C. *What Is Education?* Ginn 1916.

O'Shea, M. V. *Education as Adjustment.* Longmans 1903.

Park, R. E. and Burgess, E. W. *Introduction to the Science of Sociology.* University of Chicago Press 1921.

Parker, S. C. *Methods of Teaching in High Schools.* Ginn 1920.

Parker, S. C. *General Methods of Teaching in Elementary Schools.* Ginn 1922.

Patten, S. N. *New Basis of Civilization.* Macmillan 1907.

Phelps, W. L. *Teaching in School and College.* Macmillan 1912.

Pillsbury, W. B. *Essentials of Psychology.* Macmillan 1920.

Reisner, E. H. *Nationalism and Education.* Macmillan 1922.

Riley, A., Sadler, M. E., Jackson, C. *The Religious Question in Public Education.* Longmans 1911.

Robinson, J. H. *Mind in the Making.* Harper 1921.

Robinson, J. H. *The New History.* Macmillan 1912.

Ross, E. A. *Foundations of Sociology.* Macmillan 1905.

Ross, E. A. *Principles of Sociology.* Century 1920.

Ross, E. A. *Social Control.* Macmillan 1901.

Ross, E. A. *Social Psychology.* Macmillan 1908.

Ruediger, W. C. *Principles of Education.* Houghton Mifflin 1910.

Russell, Bertrand. *Why Men Fight.* Century 1917.

Russell, J. E. *German Higher Schools.* Longmans 1905.

Russell, J. E. *Organization of Teachers.* (Pamphlet.) Teachers College 1919.

Sachs, Julius. *American Secondary School.* Macmillan 1912.

Scott, J. F. *Patriots in the Making.* Appleton 1916.

Seeley, Levi. *Common-School System of Germany.* Kellogg 1896.

Seth, James. *Study of Ethical Principles.* Scribner 1898.

Shields, T. C. *Philosophy of Education.* Catholic Education Press 1917.

Sleight, W. G. *Educational Values and Methods.* Oxford 1915.

Small, A. W. *General Sociology.* University of Chicago Press 1905.

Small, A. W. and Vincent, G. E. *Introduction to Study of Society.* American Book 1894.

Smith, W. R. *Introduction to Educational Sociology.* Houghton Mifflin 1917.

Snedden, David. *Problems of Secondary Education.* Houghton Mifflin 1917.

Snedden, David. *Sociological Determination of Educational Objectives.* Lippincott 1921.

Spencer, Herbert. *Education.* Caldwell 1912.

Spencer, Herbert. *Social Statics.* Appleton 1878.

Stephen, Leslie. *The Science of Ethics.* Smith Elder, London, 1882.

Stevenson, J. A. *Project Method of Teaching.* Macmillan 1921.

Stout, G. F. *Manual of Psychology.* 1st edition, Hinds 1899. 3rd edition, Hinds 1915.

Strayer, G. D. *Brief Course in the Teaching Process.* Macmillan 1911.

Strayer, G. D. and Norsworthy, Naomi. *How to Teach.* Macmillan 1917.

Sumner, W. G. *Folkways*. Ginn 1906.

Sutherland, Alexander. *Origin and Growth of the Moral Instinct.* 2 vols. Longmans 1898.

Thompson, F. V. *Schooling of the Immigrant.* Harper 1920.

Thorndike, E. L. *Education.* Macmillan 1912.

Thorndike, E. L. *Educational Psychology.* 3 vols. Teachers College 1913–14.

Thorndike, E. L. *Educational Psychology, Briefer Course.* Teachers College 1914.

Todd, A. J. *Primitive Family.* Putnam 1913.

Todd, A. J. *Theories of Social Progress.* Macmillan 1918.

Veblen, Thorstein. *Higher Learning in America.* B. W. Huebsch 1918.

Wallas, Graham. *The Great Society.* Macmillan 1914.

Ward, L. F. *Applied Sociology.* Ginn 1906.

Ward, L. F. *Dynamic Sociology.* 2 vols. Appleton 1911.

Wenner, G. U. *Religious Education and the Public Schools.* American Tract 1913.

Wilson, H. B. and Wilson, G. M. *Motivation of School Work.* Houghton Mifflin 1916.

Wilson, R. K. *The Province of the State.* King, London, 1911.

Wilson, Woodrow. *The State.* Heath 1918.

Woodworth, R. S. *Dynamic Psychology.* Columbia University Press 1918.

Woodworth, R. S. *Psychology.* Holt 1921.

PERIODICALS

American Journal of Sociology. University of Chicago Press.

American Schoolmaster. State Normal College, Ypsilanti, Michigan.

Atlantic Monthly. Atlantic Monthly Company, Boston.

Catholic Educational Association Bulletins. Catholic Education Association, Columbus, Ohio.

Educational Administration and Supervision. Warwick and York, Baltimore.

Educational Review. G. H. Doran Company, New York.

Elementary School Journal. University of Chicago Press.

English Journal. University of Chicago Press.

Francis Parker School Studies in Education. Chicago.

Journal of Education. Boston.

Journal of Educational Method. World Book Co., Yonkers, N. Y.

National Education Association Proceedings. Washington, D. C.

National Society for the Study of Education. Yearbook. Public School Publishing Company, Bloomington, Ill.

Religious Education. Religious Education Association, Chicago.

School and Society. Science Press, Garrison, N. Y.

School Science and Mathematics. Smith and Turton, Mount Morris, Ill.

School and Home Education. Public School Publishing Company, Bloomington, Ill.

School Review. University of Chicago Press.

Teachers College Record. Teachers College, New York.

Teaching. Kansas State Normal School, Emporia.

United States Bureau of Education Bulletins. Washington, D. C.

1. THE MEANING OF THE PHILOSOPHY OF EDUCATION

1. What if any educational disputes do you think John Wesley and Voltaire would engage in if alive to-day?

2. If the different points of view of Thomas Jefferson and Napoleon Bonaparte were worked out in thoroughgoing consistency, in what details of education would they differ? In what agree?

3. Can you give any striking instance, ancient or modern, where any group has sought to introduce or maintain or spread any social or political regime by means of education? Was the reliance placed on curriculum or on method? Could democracy consistently approve the instances you cite?

4. What if any life interests outside of education make demands upon education? Do any of these demands conflict? If so, what then?

5. Name within the field of education some conflict which is related to a conflict outside.

6. Which precedes, experience or reflection? Always? How? Discuss the thesis:—experience : reflection :: philosophy : life :: philosophy of education : education.

7. Name in each of the following a typical problem that belongs but little if any to either of the others: philosophy of education, educational administration, the science of teaching.

8. How many people have philosophies? Have you one?

9. What is meant by the philosophy of education? Would this question come better at the close of the course?

BIBLIOGRAPHY

Source Quotations: 18*, 355, 411; 151*, 180*, 181, 412; 166*; 406*, 40*, 116, 185*, 103, 108*, 225, 390, 402b.

Monroe, *Cyclopedia of Education: Philosophy* of Education.

Dewey, *Democracy and Education*, Chap. 24.

Moore, *What Is Education*, Chap. 1.

Dewey, *How We Think*, pp. 12–13, Chap. 11.

Scott, *Patriots in the Making*, Chap. 9.

Bagley, *Educative Process*, pp. 161–165.

James, *Some Problems of Philosophy*, Chap. 1.

MacVannel, *Outlines of a Course in Philosophy of Education*, Chaps. 1, 2.

Cubberley, *Readings in the History of Education* (see index).

Betts, *Social Principles of Education*, Chap. 1.

Reisner, *Nationalism and Education*, pp. 17–28, 36–38, 51–54, 75–76, 86–87, 124–130, 139–150.

Shields, *Philosophy of Education* (Introduction).

2. EXPERIENCE AND ACTION

1. In the tiger story (S.Q. No. 53b) point out a clear-cut instance each of mechanism, drive, preparatory reaction, consummatory reaction.

2. How typical is the foregoing of animal life? Of human life? Where in terms of this analysis do you place: end (or aim), means, control, purpose, interest, thinking, choice?

3. Can you fit Woodworth's conception and terminology with Thorndike's?

4. Suppose a fierce dog is approaching, are the several things (experiences) that might happen equally desirable? If the opposite held here (and generally of analogous situations), wherein would the world of affairs be different?

5. In the experience with the dog (Q. 4) how does the past function? What say you to anything which does not function at all in experience?

6. Are the elements (things) in the situation of Q. 4 movable at your option? All? None? Some? Equally? How so? How important is this fact?

7. What does it mean that a certain contemplated evil is *avoidable?* Is avoidability a fact? Always? Ever? When and how? In the light of these considerations (including Q. 6) what is the meaning of inevitable, contingent, optional?

8. How much of life activity and experience proceeds on the principles assumed here in questions 1, 2, 4, 6, and 7? Must these principles be assumed?

9. What if any light is thrown by the foregoing on the meaning of: value, effort, control, freedom, possibility, thinking?

10. Can you now better analyze the notions of activity and experience? What is the difference between the two?

BIBLIOGRAPHY

Source Quotations: 53* (a, b, c); 325, 318*; 262, 307; 8, 98; 65, 117*, 329*.

Woodworth, *Dynamic Psychology*, pp. 36–43.

Thorndike, *Educational Psychology*, Vol. I, pp. 6–8, 123–125, Chap. 14 or *Briefer Course*, Chap. 1.

Woodworth, *Psychology*, pp. 68–82.

Dewey, *Democracy and Education*, pp. 12 *ff.*, 163–169, 177, 396 *ff.*

Conklin, *Heredity and Environment*, pp. 65–78, 459–87, 1st ed. (or 48–56, 309–323 3d ed.)

3. THE NATURE OF INSTITUTIONS

1. Where in the Woodworth analysis (Topic 2, Q. 1) may problems typically arise? What help here from Dewey's phrase "a forked road situation" (*How We Think*, p. 11)? What is the function of the solution?

2. May a problem be a social affair? In what senses may a solution be social?

3. Can a solution undergo change? Might it have a history? Does it improve or deteriorate with use?

4. If the difficult aspect of a situation recur, can the solution be used over again? Can it be passed on to another person?

5. What is a "trial and error" solution? Can it be socially made? What other kind of solution can there be? Are both kinds equally characteristic of all grades of society?

6. To what extent does the conception of "ready to use" trial and error solutions apply to household implements, to grammatical forms, to moral codes, to common law, to statute law?

7. Define and discriminate in terms of the foregoing: custom, habit, institution, civilization.

8. Where do solutions abide when not in use and in what state?

9. What bearing has Q. 8 on the nature of the educative process?

10. In terms of the foregoing define the aim of education. Do you get here any suggestion for method?

BIBLIOGRAPHY

> *Source Quotations:* 319*, 58*, 22.
> Dewey, *Democracy and Education*, pp. 169–177.
> Woodworth, *Dynamic Psychology*, pp. 27 *f.*, 90 *f.*
> Monroe, *Cyclopedia of Education:* Ability, custom, experience, problem, social heredity, educational psychology, study, thought, tradition.
> Cooley, *Social Organization*, Chap. 28.
> Ross, *Principles of Sociology*, p. 485.
> Hayes, *Introduction to Sociology*, pp. 344 *f.*, 389–394, 405 *ff.*
> Sumner, *Folkways*, pp. 2 *ff.*
> Butler, *Meaning of Education*, pp. 32–35.
> Dewey and Tufts, *Ethics*, Chap. 4.
> Ross, *Social Psychology*, Chaps. 12, 13 (customs).
> Colvin, *Learning Process*, Chaps. 1, 2 (trial and error).
> Bagley, *Educative Process*, Chaps. 1, 10, pp. 151–152.
> Colvin and Bagley, *Human Behavior*, pp. 26–35 (trial and error).
> Henderson, *Principles of Education*, pp. 96–98, 144–162, Chap. 7.

Giddings, *Theory of Human Society*, p. 174.
MacVannel, *Philosophy of Education*, Chaps. 7, 10.
Betts, *Social Principles of Education*, Chap. 5.
Giddings, *Elements of Sociology*, pp. 282–89.
Kirkpatrick, *Fundamentals of Child Study*, pp. 81–83.

4. THE SOCIAL INHERITANCE

1. What is the difference between the biological inheritance and the social inheritance? Are both peculiar to man?

2. In how many ways do the two inheritances interact?

3. Is an ax a part of the social inheritance? Is a sneeze? A wink? The Hudson River?

4. How do you connect the social inheritance with any of our previous discussions?

5. What aspects are severally emphasized by the following synonyms of the term social inheritance: social tradition, spiritual inheritance, fabric of human achievement, civilization, funded capital of civilization, capitalized experience?

6. Does the content of the social inheritance change? If yes, for better or for worse? Always?

7. In what two different senses may we speak of the continuance of society?

8. What is the relation of the social inheritance to the present status and continued existence of society?

9. How valuable is the social inheritance?

10. What keeps the social inheritance in existence?

11. In terms of the foregoing, define education.

BIBLIOGRAPHY

Source Quotations: 227*; 115*, 1c9, 282, 366; 220 (1).
Dewey, *Democracy and Education*, p. 11, Chap. 2.
Butler, *Meaning of Education*, pp. 21–38.
Baldwin, *Social and Ethical Interpretation*, Chap. 2.
Woodworth, *Dynamic Psychology*, p. 26 f.
Ellwood, *Social Psychology*, pp. 128–138.
Monroe, *Cyclopedia of Education:* Heredity, tradition, art, social psychology, psychology of language.
Hobhouse, *Social Evolution and Political Theory*, pp. 34–39.
Conn, *Social Heredity*, pp. 24–43, 298–304.
Horne, *Philosophy of Education*, pp. 97–102, 138–142, 145–147, 150 ff.
Burgess, *Function of Socialization*, pp. 21–25, 37.
Bagley, *Educative Process*, Chaps. 1, 2.
Cooley, *Social Organization*, Chap. 28.
Ross, *Social Psychology*, Chap. 12.
Ross, *Principles of Sociology*, Chap. 4.
MacVannel, *Philosophy of Education*, Chap. 6.
Cooley, *Social Process*, Chap. 18.

Dealey, *Sociology*, Chap. 3.
Ellwood, *The Social Problem*, Chap. 2.
Betts, *Social Principles of Education*, pp. 13–30, 133–148.
Moore, *What Is Education?* pp. 143 *ff*.

5. THE NATURE OF SOCIETY

1. Do birds feeding together in a flock coöperate? Geese migrating?
   Wolves hunting? People riding in a trolley-car? The totality of
   the car company's men? Boys playing ball?

2. How many can coöperate to one end? How few? For how long a
   time? How short? With how little conscious intent? With how
   much? What besides conscious intent might similarly vary in
   connection? What is included in the term coöperation?

3. How does a common purpose differ from mere group consciousness?
   Had Jacob and Esau a common purpose as regards Isaac's bless-
   ing? David and Jonathan as regards Saul's evil intent? How
   many purposes (more or less active) are you now sharing with
   others? With how many others?

4. How do you define association (i.e., a social organization)? Do
   questions 1, 2, or 3 help?

5. In how many associations might one have simultaneous member-
   ship? Are such associations cause or effect as regards people's
   wish to commingle?

6. Show how purposes shared in larger or smaller groupings link the
   people of a village together. How is it with the people of a nation?
   The people of the world in 1920? In 1420?

7. Name some instincts and other factors that most of all have
   brought people together in society or now so hold them.

8. Do the works of a running watch represent a state of society?
   Does a herd of buffaloes? A hive of bees? A prison full of men
   in solitary confinement? A number of neighboring hermits? The
   dwellers in a New York apartment house? A tribe of Indians?
   The people of Holland? What do you mean by a state of society?
   Do questions 5 and 6 help?

9. Analyze the conception of a state of society in such a way as to
   show its essential implications.

10. How do you relate association, society, social inheritance, and
    education?

BIBLIOGRAPHY

Source Quotations: 89*, 169, 328, 128; 57*; 388, 365*, 59*, 385, 78, 275;
125; 148; 153, 304.
Dewey, *Democracy and Education*, Chaps. 1, 2, 7.
Baldwin, *Individual and Society*, Chaps. 1, 2, 3.
Cooley, *Social Organization*, Chap. 1.
Maciver, *Community*, pp. 5–7, 22 *ff.*, 180 *ff.*

Woodworth, *Dynamic Psychology*, Chap. 8.
Giddings, *Elements of Sociology*, pp. 5 *ff.*, 100–102, Chap. 7.
Giddings, *Principles of Sociology*, Bk. II, Chap. 2, pp. 114–116, 172;
    Bk. IV, Chap. 4.
Park and Burgess, *Introduction to the Science of Sociology*, pp. 27–43.
MacDougall, *Social Psychology*, Chap. 10.
Betts, *Social Principles of Education*, Chap. 2.
Hayes, *Introduction to Sociology*, pp. 302, 417–424.
Ross, *Social Control*, Chap. 9.
Bagehot, *Physics and Politics*, pp. 51–52.
Cooley, *Human Nature and the Social Order*, Chap. 1.
Ellwood, *Social Psychology*, pp. 5 *ff.*, 33 *f.*, 39 *ff.*, 79 *ff.*, 323–328.
Ellwood, *Sociology in Its Psychological Aspects* (see index).
Fite, *Individualism*, pp. 98 *ff.*
MacVannel, *Philosophy of Education*, Chap. 6.
Blackmar and Gillen, *Outlines of Sociology*, Chap. 1.
Small and Vincent, *Introduction to Study of Society*, Bk. I, Chap. 5;
    Bk. V, Chaps. 1, 2.
Baldwin, *Dictionary:* Social consciousness, social unit, sociology.

6. SOCIALIZATION—I

1. Seeing that man is by instinct already "social," what can a process of socialization mean?

2. Show how a baby's milk bottle may help the infant in his early steps towards socialization.

3. What is the relation of the social inheritance to the process of socialization? Name several tools, implements, and institutions that have little or no socializing effect.

4. What is Dewey's criterion for the ethical evaluation of an association? (*Democracy and Education*, p. 95 *f.*)

5. To which does socialization properly apply: to individuals, to the whole group, to sub-groups? Does the conception hold as between nations? Does Dewey's criterion apply?

6. What relationships with socialization have: morality, politeness, tolerance, invention?

7. To what extent is all the foregoing cared for under the concept of sharing (the sharing of interests, activities and relationships)?

8. What if any light does the foregoing throw on a proper meaning of "Americanization"?

9. What if any educational objectives emerge from the discussion of Topics 5 and 6?

10. What suggestions do you get from all the foregoing for determining school procedure and the content of the curriculum?

BIBLIOGRAPHY

Source Quotations: 52*, 128, 302.
Dewey, *Democracy and Education*, pp. 7–8, 15–16, 96–102, 414–417.
Burgess, *Function of Socialization* (especially the Introduction).
Giddings, *Elements of Sociology*, Chaps. 5, 6.
Giddings, *Theory of Socialization.*
Dewey, *School and Society*, Chap. 1.
MacVannel, *Philosophy of Education*, pp. 113–116, 146–151.
Cooley, *Social Organization*, Chaps. 11, 14.
Dewey, *Schools of Tomorrow*, Chaps. 9, 10.
Dewey and Tufts, *Ethics* (Index: socializing process and agencies).
Ellwood, *Introduction to Social Psychology*, pp. 166, 310.
Ellwood, *Sociology in Its Psychological Aspects*, pp. 235–245.
Betts, *Social Principles in Education*, pp. 14–18, 291–293.
Dewey, *Moral Principles in Education*, Chaps. 2, 3, 4.
Fite, *Individualism*, p. 104.
Monroe, *Cyclopedia of Education:* Knowledge, information.
Kirkpatrick, *Individual in the Making*, Chaps. 5, 7.

7. THE NATURE OF THE INDIVIDUAL

1. What light does Topic 2 throw on the nature of man?

2. What additional in the lamb would make its fattening for slaughter a wrong?

3. What is meant by a self? What if any light from Q. 2?

4. Contrast "internal" with "external" (coerced) choices. What further light on the self? What light on the meaning of self-expression?

5. What does self-expression mean in the case of the drug addict? The dissipated man? The choleric man? The contented slave? The ignoramus? The child? Are there degrees of self-expression? Does the notion of self-realization help here? What are the mutual relationships of self-expression and self-realization?

6. What is the meaning of Kant's dictum: "So act as to treat humanity, whether in thine own person or in that of any other, in every case as an end withal, never as a means merely"? Illustrate.

7. What is meant by respect for personality? For the personality of the drug addict? Of the angry man? The criminal? The ignoramus? The child? The normal man of thirty? Any light here from Q. 6?

8. Can you define selfishness in terms of a "narrow" self as opposed to a "broad" self?

9. Who is free? A criminal in prison? Epictetus in prison? The drug addict? An angry man? The prejudiced man? A contented slave? An indoctrinated man? A person with convictions? A child? Aristotle in his prime? What senses of the term free do you distinguish? Do questions 5 and 6 help?

BIBLIOGRAPHY

> *Source Quotations:* 1, 386, 49; 359, 395; 288*; 2, 291*, 193; 293*, 85, 187; 70, 376*; 337, 145, 135, 413.
> Dewey, *Democracy and Education*, pp. 52–3, 62, 98, 295, 408 *ff*.
> Berkson, *Theories of Americanization*, pp. 24 *ff*.
> Woodworth, *Dynamic Psychology*, pp. 36 *ff*., 40 *ff*., 52 *ff*., 125–127.
> Betts, *Social Principles of Education*, Chap. 9.
> Monroe, *Cyclopedia of Education:* Individuality, Self, Personality.
> Dewey and Tufts, *Ethics*, Chaps. 17, 18, pp. 437 *ff*.
> *Cooley, *Human Nature and the Social Order*, Chaps. 5, 6, 10.
> James, *Psychology*, Vol. I, pp. 291–6, 313–6, 400–401 (*Brief course*, Chap. 12).
> MacVannel, *Philosophy of Education*, pp. 113–116.
> Angell, *Psychology*, Chap. 23.

Fite, *Introductory Study of Ethics*, Chap. 11.
>Drever, *Instincts in Man*, Chap. 11.
>Baldwin, *Individual and Society*, pp. 24 *ff.*
Coe, *Social Theory of Religious Education*, pp. 44–45.
Pillsbury, *Essentials of Psychology*, Chap. 17.
Stout, *Manual of Psychology*, pp. 527–530, 534 (1st edition).
Baldwin, *Dictionary:* Self, Person, etc.
Horne, *Philosophy of Education*, pp. 30–34.
Mackenzie, *Manual of Ethics*, pp. 95–98, 291–292, 374–375.

8. THE SOCIAL NATURE OF THE INDIVIDUAL

1. To what extent is the individual dependent on others for his physical existence and well-being?

2. How do the concepts (notions) of "ego" and "alter," self and "socius" by their constant interaction help each other into fuller being? How long does this process continue?

3. From Q. 2 what do you conclude as to the social nature of the self? Does the self thus formed affect my conduct? Illustrate.

4. What instincts especially demand relations with one's fellows?

5. How much knowledge is social in origin? In bearing? What that is entirely non-social can you learn about a stone?

6. In what respects and to what extent is one's mind social in origin?

7. How much of morality is social in origin? In bearing?

8. What kind of persons would we be without the social contribution? Which owes more to others, the Manhattanite of 1600 or one of 1900?

9. What if any light does Topic 7 throw upon this topic? This topic on Topic 7? What are the mutual relations of socialization and individualization?

10. Can you generalize from the foregoing?

BIBLIOGRAPHY

Source Quotations: 331, 109*; 302, 125; 30, 37; 303, 16e; 52, 90, 115*, 366; 62*, 346, 304; 129*, 222, 63.

Dewey, *Democracy and Education*, Chap. 2, 22, pp. 407 *ff*.

Thorndike, *Educational Psychology*, Vol. I, Chap. 7.

Woodworth, *Dynamic Psychology*, Chap. 8.

MacDougall, *Social Psychology*, pp. 174–201.

Ross, *Principles of Sociology*, pp. 41–51, 105 *ff*.

Baldwin, *Individual and Society*, Chaps. 1, 2.

Berkson, *Theories of Americanization*, pp. 34 *ff*.

Giddings, *Theory of Human Society*, pp. 227 *f*.

Baldwin, *Social and Ethical Interpretations*, Chaps. 1, 2.

Monroe, *Cyclopedia of Education:* Self.

Coe, *Social Theory of Religious Education*, pp. 122 *ff*.

Todd, *Theories of Social Progress*, Chaps. 4, 5.

Stout, *Manual of Psychology*, pp. 649–654 (3rd edition).

Dewey and Tufts, *Ethics*, Chap. 20.

Pillsbury, *Essentials of Psychology*, Chap. 17.

Ellwood, *Sociology in Its Psychological Aspects*, Chaps. 7, 10, 11.

Fite, *Individualism*, Section 1 *ff*., pp. 98 *ff*.

Cooley, *Human Nature and the Social Order*, Chaps. 3, 5, 6, 10.

MacVannel, *Philosophy of Education*, Chaps. 6, 8.
Hastings, *Encyclopedia of Religion and Ethics:* Alter.
Coe, *Psychology of Religion*, pp. 140–143.
Kirkpatrick, *The Individual in the Making*, Chap. 5.
Maciver, *Community*, p. 85.
Brown, *Underlying Principles of Modern Legislation*, pp. 111–118.
Burgess, *Function of Socialization*, Chap. 11 (see Index).

9. THE INDIVIDUAL AND SOCIETY I

1. If a farmer buys a plow, which profits, the farmer or the merchant? Which loses?

2. Do parents in caring for their children expect a "quid pro quo" from them? Does the honest man demand a "quid pro quo" each time he acts honestly?

3. How do you contrast the motivation of mutual exchange (as of Q. 1) with that of serial transfer (as of Q. 2)?

4. On which of the two bases (exchange of goods or serial transfer) do the following take place: courtesy, dinner parties, brokerage, patriotism, conservation, charity, public education, good government, eugenics?

5. What is the difference between the reasons for approving a social practice and the motivation which induces one to perform it? What is the motivation in a well-established case of serial transfer?

6. Which is older in the race history (mutual) exchange of goods or serial transfer? Which lends itself less readily to selfishness? Do we seek the happiness of another as a means to our own happiness? May one find happiness in seeking the happiness of another?

7. If a man be not disposed to continue a socially useful serial transfer series, what can society do? Will punishment serve? Might education help?

8. What bearing have the foregoing on selfishness as the basis of group life? What bearing has the whole discussion on the relation of the individual to society?

9. Is democracy concerned in the foregoing? Is education a factor?

BIBLIOGRAPHY

Source Quotations: 80, 407; 16 (a, b, d, e); 248, 128*, 140, 157, 285.
Dewey, *Democracy and Education*, pp. 407–4c9, Chap. 7.
Dewey and Tufts, *Ethics*, Chap. 3, sec. 3; Chap. 18.
Baldwin, *Individual and Society*, Chap. 3.
Giddings, *Principles of Sociology*, pp. 383–399.
MacDougall, *Social Psychology*, Chaps. 7, 8.
James, *Principles of Psychology*, Vol. I, pp. 317–329.
Cooley, *Human Nature and the Social Order*, Chap. 6.
MacVannel, *Philosophy of Education*, pp. 104–115.
Coffin, *Socialized Conscience*, Chap. 3.
Sutherland, *Origin and Growth of the Moral Instinct*, Vol. I, pp. 24–40.
Ellwood, *Sociology in Its Psychological Aspects*, Chaps. 14, 15.
Mackenzie, *Manual of Ethics*, Bk. II, Chaps. 4, 5.
Dole, *Ethics of Progress*, Part I.

Fite, *Introductory Study of Ethics*, pp. 78–94, Chap. 7.
Seth, *Study of Ethical Principles*, Part I, Chap. 3.
Mezes, *Ethics*, pp. 66 *ff*.
Bradley, *Ethical Studies*, Essay 7.

10. ACTIVITY LEADING TO FURTHER ACTIVITY

1. Do you see any significance for growth in Thorndike's neurones of secondary connection? How is satisfaction involved?

2. Is activity that suggests further activity found equally in man and brute? In all individual men? At all periods of life? How is its presence related to the quality ("worthwhileness," "satisfyingness") of life?

3. Can you explain on the basis of the foregoing why some old men find life so inane? Why you value some new thoughts above others; some books above others; some teachers above others? Why we object to "indulgence," "mere excitement," "mere pleasure"?

4. Does "further activity" refer to new acts or to a repetition of the same act? To one straight line of acts or to a branching effect of activity? To activity of the original agent or of others?

5. What are the comparative effects on "further activity" of love and hate? Of truth and falsehood? Of dissipation and "innocent pleasures"? Of marriage and profligacy? Of selfishness and unselfishness? Of good and evil?

6. How far will this conception go towards defining right and wrong? What light does it throw on culture (as an aim), happiness, education?

7. Name some activities that at first "lead on," but ultimately hinder action. Do such contradict the reasoning of Q. 5?

8. In this conception is the present subordinated to the future or the future to the present? How should it be? To grow most between 40 and 50 what should one do about growing between 10 and 20?

9. Are all activities equally apt to "lead on"? How about playing dolls, swinging, reading, playing dominoes, algebra, playing chess, reading the Elsie books, reading history, playing bridge, dramatics, "shooting craps," playing store? Does variety help?

10. How would you connect the terms: growing, education, "leading on," life?

BIBLIOGRAPHY

Source Quotations: 4: 311; 384*, 8, 141, 228*; 358*, 356*; 326, 393*, 12, 9, 14; 6.
Dewey, *Interest and Effort in Education*, pp. 35-44.
Dewey, *Democracy and Education*, Chap. 4.
Russell, *Why Men Fight*, pp. 118-128, 137 *f*., 143-146, 230-232.
Dewey and Tufts, *Ethics*, pp. 263 *ff*., 275 *ff*., 287 *ff*.

Thorndike, *Educational Psychology*, Vol. I, pp. 131, 141–2, 307–9 (*Briefer Course*, pp. 64–5).
Bonser, *Elementary School Curriculum*, Chaps. 2, 6.
MacDougall, *Social Psychology*, pp. 154 *ff*.
MacVannel, *Philosophy of Education*, p. 113 *f*.

11. THE INDIVIDUAL AND SOCIETY II

1. Does social relationship express or repress? Always?

2. Does a proper moral code repress or express? Either or neither or both? Always? Ever? When? Why?

3. What is the intent of the proper moral code: to change or to preserve man's original nature? Why?

4. What does it mean (S. Q. No. 111) that right and wrong are "in the nature of things"? What things? Can there be a "penalty" to "pay," if each follows his conscience? If people know no better? If people follow the best insight of their time?

5. In seeking an end (see Topic 7, Q. 1) is one striving to complete (and thus satisfy) the impulse (already thus begun) toward the end? Or is one seeking the satisfaction (pleasure) which the attained end will supposedly bring? Either or neither or both? What bearing here on the source of (a sense) of value?

6. How far will the conceptions of self-realization, self-expression, and respect for personality, considered in the light of Topic 10 and of questions 4, 5, 6, and 7 above, go towards determining what constitutes right and wrong?

7. Wherein would the good life as contemplated in Q. 6 differ from other ideals of the good life (e. g. S. Q. Nos. 16a*, b, 68*, 70d, 71, 74*, 86*, 95*, 96, 98, 99*, 113, 118, 124*, 126*, 130, 189, 190, 192, 226*.)

8. What if any advantage is it to have a scientific (objective) basis for determining right or wrong? Has Q. 4 any pertinence here?

9. In the light of the foregoing, what is the relation of the individual to the group? What, accordingly, is the aim in moral education?

BIBLIOGRAPHY ·

Source Quotations: 328, 157, 327*, 303; 19, 20, 394*; 52; 404*, 203, 223, 188, 352, 367; 97, 11; 356*, 306*, 246, 60*, 329, 363; 62, 385, 129, 346, 347, 16 (a, d, e, f, g), 64.

Dewey, *Democracy and Education*, pp. 123–124, 340, 356 *ff.*, 381 *ff.*

Dewey and Tufts, *Ethics*, pp. 184 *ff.*, 298 *ff.*, 362, 395 *ff.*, 428–449, 483.

Cooley, *Social Organization*, Chaps. 28–30.

MacVannel, *Philosophy of Education*, pp. 100 *ff.*, 114 *ff.*, 117 *ff.*, 146 *ff.*

Monroe, *Cyclopedia of Education:* Conduct, Character.

Maciver, *Community*, pp. 67 *ff.*, 148–161, 214–216, 218 *ff.*, 237 *ff.*

Ellwood, *Sociology in Its Psychological Aspects*, pp. 359–365, 390–395.

Hobhouse, *Social Evolution and Political Theory*, Chap. 9.

Hobhouse, *Liberalism*, Chap. 7.

Jordan, *Footnotes to Evolution*, pp. 297, 277.

McKechnie, *The State and the Individual*, Chap. 3.
Baldwin, *The Individual and Society*, pp. 13 *ff.*
Smith, *Educational Sociology*, pp. 26 *ff.*, 184 *ff.*
Fite, *Individualism*, pp. 3 *ff.*, 135 *ff.*
Bachman, *Principles of Elementary Education*, Chaps. 1, 2.
Dole, *Ethics of Progress*, Pt. I, Chap. 3; Pt. V, Chap. 3; Pt. VII, Chap.
  5.
Fite, *Introductory Study of Ethics*, Chaps. 16, 17.
Stephen, *The Science of Ethics*, Chap. 10.
Mackenzie, *Manual of Ethics*, pp. 232–244, 325–327.
Fairbanks, *Introduction to Sociology*, Chaps. 5, 9.

12. DEMOCRACY

1. To what aspects of social life, additional to government, does democracy especially pertain? What are the principal implications of democracy?

2. Can you, using our previous discussions, give one inclusive definition of democracy?

3. What should be the democratic attitude toward innate individual differences?

4. Can democracy consistently reward superior achievement? If no, how secure proper effort? If yes, what rule do you lay down?

5. What are the respective advantages of democracy and of enlightened despotism (or oligarchy)? Which do you prefer? Why?

6. Is it democratic for the present to bind the future? In all respects? In no respects? Forever? For how long? What about bond issues? Constitutions? Perpetual charters? The Dartmouth College decision?

7. How far reaching in its effect is the wider principle invoked in S. Q. No. 46?

8. Name some conditions external to a country that might oppose the realization of democracy within the country. Name some internal conditions that might prove similarly hurtful.

9. Does the action of the democratic principle stop at the national border?

10. Is democracy a theory, a fact, a faith, or a program? Which? How so?

BIBLIOGRAPHY

Source Quotations: 88, 271, 272*, 54, 278, 312, 120, 290; 347, 376*; 133; 23*, 292; 339, 137*, 172, 171*, 296*, 276*; 177*, 357; 305*, 371, 277; 334*.

Dewey, *Democracy and Education*, pp. 94–102 (also see Index).
Giddings, *Elements of Sociology*, Chap. 24.
Butler, *True and False Democracy*, Chap. 1.
Russell, *Why Men Fight*, pp. 135 ff.
Addams, *Democracy and Social Ethics*, Chaps. 1, 7.
Hobhouse, *Liberalism*, Chaps. 2, 8, 9.
Giddings, *Democracy and Empire*, Chaps. 1, 6, 12.
Dewey and Tufts, *Ethics*, pp. 550–554.
Cooley, *Social Organization*, Chaps. 5, 11, 14, 15.
Cooley, *Social Process* (see Index).
Berkson, *Theories of Americanisation*, pp. 21–45.
Smith, *Educational Sociology*, pp. 166–170.

Abbott, *The Spirit of Democracy*, Chap. 2.
Bryce, *American Commonwealth* (see Index).
Bryce, *Modern Democracies*, Vol. I, Chaps. 5, 6, 7; Vol. II, Chap. 74, pp. 550 *f.*, pp. 562 *f.*
MacVannel, *Philosophy of Education*, Chap. 9.
Dole, *The American Citizen*, Chaps. 8, 9, 23.
Faguet, *The Cult of Incompetence* (see Index).
Brown, *Underlying Principles of Modern Legislation*, pp. 314 *ff.* (also see Table of Contents).
Barker, *Political Thought from Spencer to Today* (see Index).
Blackmar and Gillen, *Sociology*, Part IV, Chaps. 5, 6, pp. 390–391.
Croly, *The Promise of American Life*, pp. 195 *ff.*
Ross, *Foundations of Sociology* (see Index).

13. DEMOCRACY AND EDUCATION

1. Is it possible for one to be so trained that the responses thus ingrained remain practically permanent? To what extent would this give the trainer power over the trained? Is Q. 9, Topic 7, pertinent?

2. How do you contrast "training" (as defined above) with "education" (broadly defined)? Might "education" include training along specific lines? How do you contrast this kind of training with "training" (as defined in Q. 1)?

3. Do habits enslave or free? All habits?

4. In terms of the foregoing what can freedom in thinking mean?

5. Wherein would a democracy and an autocracy (or caste system) take different attitudes toward "training" and "education"?

6. Is self-realization involved in "training" *vs.* "education"? Is self-expression? Respect for personality? Activity leading to further activity?

7. What was the older military ideal of a properly trained private soldier? The partisan idea of party loyalty? Of indoctrination?

8. To what if any degree is "training" necessary to a proper social state?

9. What if any adverse bearing on the working of democratic education have the accepted facts as to the distribution of intelligence.

10. In the light of all the foregoing formulate the principal demands of democracy upon American education.

BIBLIOGRAPHY

Source Quotations: 116*, 37*, 195, 196, 409; 249; 313*, 251*, 330, 19, 20; 207*, 250; 40, 21, 138*, 180, 147*, 151, 393, 185, 349; 161*, 134, 226, 144; 24*, 167; 315*, 133; 406, 265*, 288.

Dewey, *Democracy and Education*, pp. 15-16, 35 *ff.*, 225–227, Chaps. 7, 8, 9.

Religious Education, 14: 123–147 (Kilpatrick and Coe, "Education of Adolescents for Democracy").

Dewey, *Schools of Tomorrow*, pp. 303 *ff.*

Russell, *Why Men Fight*, pp. 154–168, 176–181.

Cooley, *Social Organization*, pp. 237, Chap. 4.

Goddard, *Human Efficiency and Levels of Intelligence*, pp. 95–99.

Cubberley, *Changing Conceptions in Education*, Chap. 3.

Addams, *Democracy and Social Ethics*, Chaps. 6, 7.

Robinson, *Mind in the Making*, pp. 220 *ff.*

Thorndike, *Education for Initiative and Originality*, Teachers College
  Bulletin, Series 11, No. 4.   (Reprint from *Teachers College Record*,
  17:405-16.)
Dewey and Tufts, *Ethics*, pp. 548-56.
Monroe, *Cyclopedia of Education:* Democracy and Education.
Ross, *Social Control*, pp. 172-179.
Bryce, *Modern Democracies*, Vol. I, Chap. 8.
Betts, *Social Principles of Education*, pp. 79-85.
Eliot, *Educational Reform*, Chap. 18.
Butler, *True and False Democracy*, Chap. 3.
Abbott, *Spirit of Democracy*, Chaps. 5, 6.
Hadley, *Education of the American Citizen*, pp. 17-33, 135-160
Blackmar and Gillen, *Sociology*, Part IV, Chap. 4.
Gillette, *Vocational Education*, Chap. 5.
Giddings, *Democracy and Empire*, Chaps. 12, 13, 14.
Henderson, *Principles of Education* (see Index).

14. DEMOCRACY AND THE SCHOOL

1. What proportion of its children between the ages of 6 to 14 should a well-regulated democracy have in school? Why? Of its children from 15 to 18? From 19 to 24? What new considerations appear as age increases?

2. What proportion of their total annual income (not tax income) should a democratic people spend on the education of their children? How is it now?

3. In what bad sense may the word docility be used? If you wished to make men and women thus docile, how would you conduct their schooling? Do any among us wish such docile people?

4. What different attitudes should characterize a democracy and an autocracy (or a caste system) as regards: (*a*) Methods of teaching and discipline? (*b*) Methods of supervision? (*c*) Administrative procedure?

5. Can you illustrate any part of Q. 4 from American practice? From European practice?

6. What specific steps should this country take in order to approach as near as may be feasible to equality of educational opportunity?

7. Why should democracy wish vocational education? What if any are the opposed dangers? What undemocratic schemes have been proposed? What is desirable? What feasible?

8. In the light of all the foregoing what changes towards a better democracy would you advocate in American education?

BIBLIOGRAPHY

Source Quotations: 241*; 21*, 162, 173, 187; 244*, 150*, 108*, 103, 225, 116, 17; 379*, 387*, 332, 286, 353, 277, 372; 265.

Religious Education, 14:123–137 (Kilpatrick and Coe, "Education of Adolescents for Democracy").

Smith, *Educational Sociology*, Chap. 9, pp. 166 *ff.*, 217 *ff.*

American Schoolmaster, 9:14–21 (Bagley, "The Educational Basis of Democracy"). Same in *School and Home Education*, 35:147–9.

Hadley, *Freedom and Responsibility*, Chap. 7.

Addams, *Democracy and Social Ethics*, Chaps. 1, 6.

Alexander, *Prussian Elementary Schools*, Chaps. 14–29.

Ross, *Principles of Sociology*, Chap. 51.

Snedden, *Sociological Determination of Educational Objectives*, pp. 289 *ff.*

Gillette, *Vocational Education*, Chap. 5.

Reisner, *Nationalism and Education* (see Index: France, Prussia).

Seeley, *Common-School System of Germany*, Chap. 15.

Farrington, *French Secondary Schools*, Chap. 8.

Bobbitt, *The Curriculum*, Chap. 7.

Dewey, *Schools of Tomorrow*, pp. 306 *ff*.
Monroe, *Cyclopedia of Education:* Germany, Education in.
Blackmar and Gillen, *Outlines of Sociology*, Part IV, Chaps. 4, 6.
Russell, *German Higher Schools*, Chaps. 5, 6.
Howe, *Socialized Germany*, Chaps. 15, 16, 17.

15. SOCIAL CONTROL

1. Conceive a scale showing varying degrees of respect for personality. Where on this would you locate such types of social control as: fear of (popular) disapproval, habituation to subservience, (physical) force, threat of force, "training" (Topic 13), "education," desire for (popular) approval? Where would law or public opinion (considering the varying attitudes towards them) be placed? At one point or many?

2. Could you correlate with the foregoing different types of governmental and social systems? Where would anarchy belong? What is the relation of absolute personal sovereignty to social control? What has ethics to say? What parts of the scale will a democracy use? Why?

3. Could the varying attitudes of any one person in his efforts to control others be distributed on this scale? Could a group of people be analogously distributed according to their varying central tendencies in this matter of control? Could teachers (as controllers) be similarly distributed? Pupils (as controlled)? Expounders of educational theory? Types of method?

4. How does the first question in Q. 3 provide a place through education for elevating personality? What bearing here on a proper use of punishment?

5. What is meant by the tyranny of the majority? What if any ethical considerations limit the majority's right to control? What practical considerations should limit it?

6. What is meant by the irreconcilability of a sub-group? Illustrate. How is democracy concerned?

7. What do you conclude from all the foregoing as to the nature of democratic social control?

8. Do any of the foregoing considerations apply to international relations? Does ethics apply internationally? Is there such a theory as international anarchy? Who advocate it? What do you think of absolute national sovereignty?

9. What light does the foregoing discussion throw on the meaning of democracy? On the relation of education and democracy?

BIBLIOGRAPHY

Source Quotations: 150*, 297, 208, 232a, 391*, 154, 79, 185, 162, 271*, 296; 324, 242, 255; 163; 3a*, 337*, 173, 25 (a, b), 137; 50*; 156*, 48*, 261, 305, 184.

Dewey, *Democracy and Education*, Chaps. 3, 7, 9.

Ross, *Social Control*, Part I, Chaps. 1, 7, 9.
Giddings, *Theory of Human Society*, Chap. 12.
Dewey and Tufts, *Ethics*, pp. 60–61, 353–363.
Cooley, *Social Organization*, Chap. 12.
Berkson, *Theories of Americanization*, pp. 39 ff.
Ross, *Principles of Sociology*, Chaps. 34, 35.
MacDougall, *Social Psychology*, pp. 186 ff,
MacVannel, *Philosophy of Education*, pp. 146–151.
Ellwood, *Social Psychology*, Chaps. 4, 5.
Russell, *Why Men Fight*, pp. 68–78.
Patten, *New Basis of Civilization*, Chap. 8.
Baldwin, *Individual and Society*, Chap. 2.
Bryce, *Modern Democracies*, Vol. I, Chap. 6.
Hadley, *Education of the American Citizen*, pp. 135–141.
Hobhouse, *Liberalism*, Chap. 7.
Canby, *Education by Violence*.
Bryce, *American Commonwealth*, Chaps. 84, 85 (Chaps. 55, 56, abridged
    edition).
Hayes, *Introduction to Sociology*, Chap. 31.

16. MOBILIZATION OF THOUGHT POWER

1. From the analogy involved what should this topic mean? Is war necessarily suggested?

2. Does this mobilization (social utilization) refer to the stimulation, to the collection, to the organization, or to the focusing of thought? To individual thought or to group thinking?

3. What are the conditions that especially call for the mobilization of thought?

4. What more important agencies are mobilizing the thought of our country? To what more important ends?

5. How do the agencies at work along this line on this continent in 1900 compare with those of 1700? of 1400?

6. What is propagandism?* How do you contrast it with the mobilization of thought? With education?

7. How is a public opinion built (S. Q. No. 27)? What difference does popular feeling (e. g. in war) make? Do the laws of learning enter? How?

8. What dangers attend respectively the press and the moving picture as regards the matter of questions 5 and 6? What can the schools do?

9. What is the proper place of the expert in a democracy? What are the dangers? Do you approve of education for leadership? What are the dangers?

10. How is democracy concerned with this topic? What is the duty of the school? What is feasible?

BIBLIOGRAPHY

Source Quotations: 304*; 345*; 278b*, 78, 178, 165; 84; 382*, 385; 27*, 256*, 37; 176*, 348, 146, 119, 267, 235, 174, 181; 283*, 51*, 336.
Ross, *Social Control*, Chap. 10.
Russell, *Why Men Fight*, pp. 4–5.
Giddings, *Principles of Sociology*, Bk. II, Chap. 2.
Ellwood, *Sociology in Its Psychological Aspects*, Chap. 15.
Lippmann, *Public Opinion*, pp. 123–9, 320–7, 358–365.
Ross, *Social Psychology*, Chap. 22.
Cooley, *Social Organization*, Chaps. 12–15.
Wallas, *The Great Society*, pp. 240–286.
Lowell, *Public Opinion and Popular Government*, Chaps. 1, 2, 4, 17, 19.
Butler, *True and False Democracy*, Chap. 2.
Bryce, *American Commonwealth* (Index: Public opinion).
Ross, *Principles of Sociology*, Chap. 24.
Giddings, *Elements of Sociology*, Chap. 15.

Bryce, *Modern Democracies*, Vol. I, Chap. 10; Vol. II, Chap. 75.
Ward, *Applied Sociology*, pp. 43–49.
Hayes, *Introduction to Sociology*, pp. 680–684.
Todd, *Theories of Social Progress*, Chap. 25.
MacDougall, *Social Psychology*, pp. 188 *ff*.
School and Society, 4: 913–918 (Alexander, "Public Opinion and the
    Schools").
Ward, *Dynamic Sociology*, Vol. II, Chap. 12.
Atlantic Monthly, 121:62–66 (Villard, "Press Tendencies and Dangers").
Eliot, *American Contributions to Civilization*, pp. 17–33.
English Journal, 3:1–14 (Scott, "The Undefended Gate").

17. SOCIALIZATION II

1. Name some ill effects of the lack of socialization that concern our (or your) country.

2. Name some factors (geographic, biologic, economic, historic, etc.) that hinder socialization. What is the present tendency of these several factors, to increase or decrease in their effect?

3. Do any of these factors reinforce each other in their tendency towards cleavage and stratification? Why is the "automatic inheritance of allegiance" a bad thing in this connection? (S. Q. No. 77).

4. What connection do you see between socialization and the ease with which opinions spread throughout the group? Is such a spread good or evil? Always? How?

5. What personal characteristics are correlative of a proper spread of valuable ideas? What can the schools do?

6. In what respects and in what degree do we desire uniformity among the people of a group (nation)? What are the mutually opposed dangers?

7. What are some of the specific (*countable* or *measurable*) evidences that a community is not in a high degree of socialization with the rest of the country? Do the same considerations hold internationally?

8. What is the "great society"? Is it here or only coming? What are the present tendencies? How long will they continue? What light here on outstanding problems?

9. In the light of all the foregoing, what should be the policy of the educational statesman? What correlative modifications of current practice would he advocate?

BIBLIOGRAPHY

Source Quotations: 128*; 77*; 78*, 178*, 179*; 87*; 29*, 28, 153, 305, 277.

Wallas, *The Great Society*, Chap. 1.

Burgess, *The Function of Socialization in Social Evolution*, Chaps. 14, 15, pp. 172 *ff*.

Hayes, *Introduction to the Study of Sociology* Chap. 3.

Ellwood, *Sociology in Its Psychological Aspects*, Chap. 8.

Dewey, *Democracy and Education* (Index: Class Distinctions).

Giddings, *Theory of Socialisation*.

Ellwood, *Social Psychology*, pp. 95 *ff*.

Giddings, *Elements of Sociology*, Chap. 6.

Huntington and Cushing, *Human Geography*, pp. 6 *ff*., 384 *ff*.

Cooley, *Social Organization*, Chaps. 11, 12.
Ross, *Social Control* (see Index.)
School and Home Education, 35:215–218 (or *N. E. A. Proceedings*, 1916) (Bagley, "Common Elements vs. Differentiated Curricula").
School and Home Education, 34: 119–131 (Bagley, "Principles Justifying Common Elements in the School Program").
Bobbitt, *The Curriculum*, Chap. 12.
Fite, *Individualism*, p. 104, par. 67.
Ross, *Foundations of Sociology*, Chap. 9.

18. PROGRESS

1. Define most generally the meaning of social progress. Is it an affair of new and better means or of new and better ends?

2. What are some of the lines along which progress has most evidently been made? Are these equal in importance (or significance), or do some carry further than others? Which if any one line seems to be most significant?

3. Does history disclose a uniform rate of progress or are there fluctuations? Has mankind ever made any mistakes? On a large scale? Or only on a small scale? Has the rate of progress ever been reduced to zero? To a negative quantity? Illustrate.

4. Which outruns, our social problems or our social solutions? Does the disparity increase or decrease or remain constant?

5. Does gain (progress) at one point involve loss at another? Always? Ever? In such case what is the net result? Always?

6. Can endeavor control the outcome? Always? Ever? When? Has Q. 7, Topic 2, any bearing here?

7. To what extent is endeavor necessary for attaining one's ordinary aims? For (small) group aims? What added difficulty for the group? How about larger groups?

8. Is net social progress inevitable, impossible, or contingent? Which? Do the observed facts bear out your answer?

9. Under what conditions do doubt and pessimism hinder progress?

10. To what extent will progress come of itself for the individual in his own affairs? For society in its affairs? In what sense and to what degree are we responsible for progress?

BIBLIOGRAPHY

Source Quotations: 41, 42, 362; 364*, 206, 204*, 281; 122, 378, 357; 51*, 121*, 154; 361*; 231*, 262; 36, 39; 300, 299*, 340, 377, 43, 44, 35; 403*, 10; 342*, 31*, 321*, 317, 307, 209, 410.

Todd, *Theories of Social Progress*, pp. 85–112, 113–148, 505–510, 535–548.

Robinson, *The New History*, Chap. 8.

Hobhouse, *Social Evolution and Political Theory*, Chaps. 1–4, 7.

Dewey and Tufts, *Ethics*, Chap. 20.

Ellwood, *Sociology in Its Psychological Aspects*, Chap. 18 (also see Index).

Ellwood, *Social Psychology*, Chaps. 2, 13.

Giddings, *Theory of Human Society*, pp. 230–235.

Ellwood, *Sociology and Modern Social Problems*, Chaps. 2, 16.

Bagehot, *Physics and Politics*, p. 55.

Giddings, *Elements of Sociology*, Chap. 23.
Giddings, *Democracy and Empire*, Chap. 5.
Ward, *Dynamic Sociology*, Vol. II, pp. 158–211.
Ross, *Social Control* (see Index).
Smith, *Educational Sociology* (see Index).
Lowie, *Primitive Society*, pp. 433–434.
Giddings, *Principles of Sociology* (see Index).
Ward, *Applied Sociology*, pp. 21 *ff.*, Chaps. 3, 4, 11.

19. SOCIAL STABILITY IN A DYNAMIC SOCIETY

1. Name some tendencies toward social disintegration now evident in the world.

2. In a static society, what is meant by social stability? How is it maintained?

3. Does a static society differ from a dynamic (that is, plastic, changing, flexible, mobile, adaptable) society in kind or degree? Might a society be dynamic in some respects and static in others? Illustrate.

4. If a society becomes more dynamic, (*a*) In what if any respect do the following tend to change? (*b*) With what consequent effect upon social stability (or the reverse)?
Authoritarianism, coöperation, convictions (number and strength), direct action, freedom of speech, hereditary group allegiances, philosophic theory, respect for personality, socialization, status.

5. What does Small mean (S.Q. No. 106) that the intellectual interest alone is on a purely dynamic basis?

6. In the light of the foregoing what is meant by social stability in a dynamic society?

7. What do you conclude if a society becomes more dynamic, that it will become (*a*) inevitably more stable, (*b*) inevitably less stable, (*c*) contingently stable or unstable?

8. Will society become more static or more dynamic? Either? Inevitably?

9. What factors are now working against social stability in this (or your) country? What can the schools do?

BIBLIOGRAPHY

Source Quotations: 266*, 121*, 342, 107, 277; 19*, 20*; 32, 33*, 91*, 405*, 201, 204, 206, 36, 88*, 108*, 153, 105, 55; 106*; 93*; 301*, 294, 409; 155*, 274*, 259, 260, 268, 321; 207*, 265.

Ellwood, *Social Psychology*, pp. 167–8.
Dewey, *Democracy and Education*, pp. 59–65.
Ross, *Social Control*, pp. 395–410.
Ellwood, *Sociology and Modern Social Problems*, pp. 378–384.
Hayes, *Introduction to Sociology*, pp. 413–15.
Ross, *Social Psychology*, pp. 79–80.
Robinson, *The New History*, Chap. 8.
Robinson, *Mind in the Making*, pp. 179–193, Chap. 8.
Dealey, *Sociology*, pp. 67 *f*., 192 *f*.
Shields, *Philosophy of Education*, pp. 48–60.
Small, *General Sociology*, pp. 381–394, 707.

20. EDUCATION AND SOCIAL PROGRESS

1. What bearing on a theory of social progress has the question of the transmissibility of acquired characteristics? What is the educational corollary?

2. What is the best current opinion as regards innate differences in racial ability? What should we conclude as to the power and function of education?

   What are the more strategic places in our total educational system for originating progressive ideas? For spreading progressive ideas? How so? What is the practical corollary?

   How do variation and selection enter as factors in progress in the matter of ideas?

5. How does the university help most in bringing progress? Is this a democratic procedure?

6. What is academic freedom? What service does it perform? What characteristic dangers threaten academic freedom in state universities? In non-sectarian privately endowed institutions? In sectarian universities (if such can be)? How do these several types help each other? What corollary as regards a national university?

7. What effect have insistent personal interest and the laws of learning on the policies men advocate? Does a like psychology hold for the advocates of the opposed side? Which side is honest? What is the way out of this impasse? What can the impartial do? And the schools?

8. What relation to our topic have freedom of speech, freedom of press and freedom of assembly? Do we have these freedoms in America? May these freedoms be carried too far? If yes, where draw the line?

9. Within what limits can we foretell what social problems our pupils will in their time face? What personal characteristics should the schools accordingly seek to build? How go about it?

BIBLIOGRAPHY

Source Quotations: 40*; 269*; 101*; 26*; 199*, 243*, 180, 186; 25*, 201, 204, 191, 206*, 205*, 338*, 279*, 314, 202, 340, 168; 175*, 207*, 173.

Ellwood, *Social Psychology*, pp. 149 ff., 153 ff., 167 ff., 287–311.

Ellwood, *Sociology in Its Psychological Aspects*, Chap. 18.

Thorndike, *Educational Psychology*, Vol. I, pp. 231 ff., Vol. III, Chap. 10.

Ellwood, *Sociology and Modern Social Problems*, pp. 230–33; Chap. 16.

Educational Review, 58:39–58 (Finney, "Education as a Factor in Social
Progress").

Monroe, *Cyclopedia of Education:* Freedom, Academic.

Bury, *History of Freedom of Thought*, Chap. 1.

Hobhouse, *Social Evolution*, Chaps. 1, 2, 3, 4, 7.

Chafee, *Freedom of Speech*, Chap. 7.

Bagehot, *Physics and Politics*, pp. 25 *ff.*, 29, 51 *f.*, 55, 57 *f.*, 60 *f.*, 64,
102 *f.*, 156 *ff.*

Ross, *Social Control*, Chaps. 13, 14, 31.

Cooley, *Social Organization*, Chaps. 1–6.

Maciver, *Community*, pp. 174 *ff.*, 192 *ff.*

Smith, *Educational Sociology*, p. 168.

Dealey, *Sociology*, Chap. 13.

Hayes, *Introduction to Sociology*, pp. 277–282, 666–668.

Russell, *Why Men Fight*, pp. 126–130.

Veblen, *Higher Learning in America*, pp. 1–58.

Giddings, *Principles of Sociology*, Bk. III, Chap. 4 (especially pp.
347–360).

Todd, *Theories of Social Progress* (see Index).

Educational Review, 47:291–4 (Butler, "Academic Freedom").

American Journal of Sociology, 23:92–93 (Reuter, "The Superiority of
the Mulatto").

21. THE STATE AND EDUCATION

1. What different attitudes toward public education might be expected from the following: laissez faire, anarchy, socialism? What is the present dominant democratic doctrine as to the proper sphere of state action in general?

2. Should the state support schools? Why? Should they be free? Why free schools and not free bread? Does the argument hold equally of all types and grades of schooling?

3. Do free schools mean equality of opportunity? What is the democratic corollary? What feasible can we do?

4. Is it right to tax for public schools those who patronize non-public schools? Why not apportion school funds to non-public schools?

5. What principles does democracy demand in the raising and spending of school funds within a state? Do the principles apply within the federal union?

6. Does support imply control? Possibly? Inevitably? Advisably? Control in all respects? What about the proposed national bill? What is wise? Why?

7. Is compulsory attendance justifiable in a democracy? Why? Who shall decide what is a school? Does this mean state inspection of non-public schools? A state-made curriculum for them?

8. What if any proper part has the government (aside from its educational administrative machinery) in making curricula? What are the pros and cons?

9. As regards the public schools (elementary or secondary), (*a*) What if any degree of "radicalism" of opinion should debar a teacher? (*b*) In what degree if any should a teacher be restricted as regards outside participation in controversial religious, social, or political movement? (*c*) What if any attention should the school give to such controversial questions?

BIBLIOGRAPHY

Source Quotations: 232*, 360*, 391; 341*; 297*, 295, 338*; 180, 185; 207*, 173*, 191, 201, 202, 204, 205, 206*.
Cubberley, *Public School Administration*, Chap. 2.
Brown, *Underlying Principles of Modern Legislation*, pp. 1–8.
Cubberley, *School Funds and Their Apportionment*, Chaps. 1, 2; pp. 217–21.
Coe, *Social Theory of Religious Education*, Chap. 17, pp. 248 *ff.* (For titles and references, see pp. 350 *ff.*)
Dewey and Tufts, *Ethics*, Chap. 21.
Mill, *Liberty*, Chap. 4 (Opposes state systems).

Dutton and Snedden, *Administration of Public Education*, Chaps. 3, 4, 5.

Carver, *Principles of Political Economy*, Chap. 46.

Robinson, *Mind in the Making*, p. 190 *f*.

N. E. A. *Proceedings*, 1905, 111–113 (Giddings, "Compulsory Education").

Monroe, *Cyclopedia of Education:* Attendance, compulsory.

Smith, *Educational Sociology*, Chaps. 8, 12.

Russell, *Organization of Teachers* (pamphlet).

Spencer, *Social Statics* (see Table of Contents). (Opposes state systems).

Wilson, *The State*, Chaps. 3, 4.

Barker, *Political Thought from Spencer* (see Index).

Wilson, *The Province of the State*, Chaps. 4, 5; pp. 301 *ff*.

22. PRIVATE *VS.* PUBLIC EDUCATION

1. As regards the element of progress in educational thought and practice, how do you contrast public and non-public endeavor? Do all non-public schools stand on the same footing in this regard?

2. Does public education make for undesirable uniformity in our population?

3. Should public schools teach religion? If yes, how manage it? If no, why not? What should be done?

4. What is the democratic attitude as regards the parent's freedom of choice in matters educational? What is his child's right in the matter? Society's duty?

5. What if any bearing has the presence of non-public schools upon the support accorded to public schools? Is democracy concerned?

6. What principal cleavages and separating contrasts existing within American society are affected for good or ill by the type of school patronized? Do elementary, secondary, and higher education stand on the same footing in this regard? Is the automatically inherited allegiance a factor?

7. What considerations especially lead to the founding (*a*) of non-parochial private schools? (*b*) of parochial schools? Is democracy concerned? What corollary do you draw?

8. What is democracy's duty as regards schools conducted in a foreign language? What are the opposed dangers?

9. If you thought separate school systems hurtful, what steps would you advocate? What dangers would you seek to avoid?

BIBLIOGRAPHY

Source Quotations: 87*, 341; 77*; 195, 196, 270, 333*, 348*.
Dewey, *Democracy and Education*, Chap. 7.
Cubberley and Elliott, *Source Book*, Chap. 28.
Catholic Encyclopedia: Schools.
Catholic Education Bulletins: Vol. XII, No. 2 (P. R. McDevitt, "The State and Education"); Vol. XIII, No. 1 (Fenlon, "The State"; Shields, "Some Relations between the Catholic School System and the Public School System").
Betts, *Social Principles of Education*, pp. 72–79.
Monroe, *Cyclopedia of Education:* Bible in the Schools; Lutheran Church and Education in the U. S.; Parish Schools; Private Schools; Roman Catholic Church.
Dunney, *The Parish School*, Chap. 2.
Massachusetts Report of the Commission on Immigration, pp. 147–151 ("Parochial Schools").

Shields, *Philosophy of Education*, pp. 339–347.

School Review, 21:523–37 (Potter, "Relative Efficiency of Public and Private Secondary Institutions").

Thompson, *Schooling of the Immigrant*, Chap. 4.

School and Society, 4:785–786 ("Resolutions of the Catholic Educational Association").

Educational Review, 23:264–280, 511–520 (Edwards, "Private School in American Life").

Wenner, *Religious Education and the Public Schools.*

Sachs, *American Secondary School*, pp. 154–78.

Phelps, *Teaching in School and College*, Chap. 5.

Draper, *American Education*, pp. 10, 127–8, Pt. IV, Chap. 4.

Riley, Sadler, Jackson, *The Religious Question in Public Education.* *N. E. A. Proceedings*, 1890, pp. 179–85.

23. EDUCATION ITS OWN END

1. In the light of the discussion on "activity leading to further activity" what is the meaning of immaturity? Of development?

2. "There is nothing to which education is subordinate save more education." (Dewey, *Democracy and Education*, p. 60).

    a. What does this mean? What is the relation of this statement to "activity leading to further activity?"

    b. To what extent would this theory ignore subject matter and seek growth instead? How far are the two opposed?

    c. Could we on this basis have a written course of study? How specific could it be?

    d. Could children be taught in classes as now?

    e. How could we use standard tests?

3. Can present growth and preparation for future growth either oppose the other? If you wished maximum growing at the age of 40, what would you do about growing at 10, 15, 20, 25?

4. What are the ill effects of considering education as merely a preparation for life? Is education not in fact a preparation for life. When should one cease to acquire and begin to utilize his education?

5. Does this theory sufficiently consider the democratic relation of the individual to others?

6. What are the good and bad effects of such a scheme of external examinations as "the Regents'" in New York? How does the action of such a scheme fit with the thesis of this topic?

7. Why does Dewey (*Democracy and Education*, p. 89) object to finding an aim for education outside the process of education? Is his idea practicable in the world as it is to-day?

BIBLIOGRAPHY

Source Quotations: 230*; 239*, 228*, 358*, 374*, 393, 247, 309, 381, 383; 353*, 316*, 238, 335; 237.

Monroe, *Cyclopedia of Education:* Adjustment; Adaptation; Activity; Education (p. 400); Experience (p. 548); Control, Psychological.

Dewey, *Interest and Effort in Education*, pp. 35–44.

Dewey, *Democracy and Education*, pp. 63 *ff.*, 89 *ff.*, Chap. 4.

Thorndike, *Education for Initiative and Originality*, Teachers College Bulletin, Series 11, No. 4. (Reprint from *T. C. Record* 17:405–16).

MacDougall, *Social Psychology*, pp. 154 *ff.*

Dewey and Tufts, *Ethics*, pp. 263 *ff.*, 275 *ff.*, 237 *ff.*

Russell, *Why Men Fight*, pp. 118–128, 137 *ff.*, 143–146, 230–232.

24. THE NATURE OF SUBJECT MATTER

1. What are the most evident implications of the term experience? What if any relations have the experience process and the educative process?

2. The terms child and subject matter seem disparate; how nearly can you reduce them to a common denominator? What educational problem created by the disparateness now (nearly) disappears? In what new form does the problem now appear?

3. In the experience process what is the function of new subject-matter-of-attention? Of old subject matter? What are the possible relations of educational subject matter to the race experience? What is the relation of subject matter to S➤R bonds? To learning? To educational outcomes? To educational objectives?

4. Analyze the educative process among savages in such way as to disclose the nature and place therein of subject matter, teacher, method, and curriculum.

5. Do the same for the educative process of a child of 4 among us; of a man of 40, of the extra-school life of a boy of 12.

6. Do actual educational outcomes appear singly? Always? Ever? When?

7. To what extent may subject matter be removed for proper learning from its "native habitat" ("natural situation," "natural setting")? What are the related dangers? What is the common practice?

8. To what extent may desirable school subject matter be adequately and properly cared for on the basis of specific assignments? And of coercion?

9. When may subject matter be properly said to have been learned? What inadequate types or degrees of learning are common?

10. Can you in the light of the foregoing define for educational theory subject matter, curriculum, method?

BIBLIOGRAPHY

Source Quotations: 211*, 24.
Dewey, *Child and Curriculum.*
Dewey, *Democracy and Education,* pp. 158, 163–169, 177, 212–227.
Dewey, *My Pedagogic Creed.*
Teachers College Record, 22: 311–312.
McMurry, *Elementary School Standards,* Chaps. 8, 9, 10.
• Dewey, *Educational Situation,* pp. 30–49.
Monroe, *Cyclopedia of Education:* Course of Study.

Journal of Educational Method, 1:312–318, 367–374.
Teachers College Record, 16:307–338 (McMurry, "Principles Under-
  lying Making of School Curricula").
MacVannel, *Philosophy of Education*, pp. 82, 182–193.
Charters, *Methods of Teaching*, Chaps. 2–6.
Inglis, *Principles of Secondary Educatior*, pp. 394 *ff.*
Miller, *Education for the Needs of Life*, Chap. 4.
Monroe, *History of Education* (see Index).
Todd, *Primitive Family*, Chaps. 6, 7.
Spencer, *Education*, Chap. 1.
Bonser, *Elementary School Curriculum*, Chap. 1.
Bobbitt, *The Curriculum*, Chap. 6.
Betts, *Social Principles of Education*, Chap. 10.
Parker, *Methods of Teaching in High Schools*.
Earhart, *Types of Teaching*, Chap. 1.
Ruediger, *Principles of Education*, Chaps. 3–5, 10.
Snedden, *Problems of Secondary Education* (see Index).

25. THE PROBLEM OF METHOD I

1. Is method a question of how the child should act or of how the teacher should act?

2. What is the relation of method to the experience (educative) process? To subject matter? To the aim of education? What are the aims to be sought and the dangers to be avoided by good method?

3. What if any bearing on the answer to Q. 2 have the suggested distinctions of primary, associate and concomitant learning? (*Project Method*, pp. 9 *ff.*)

4. Is democracy concerned in questions 2 and 3? If so, how? Does Topic 23 enter?

5. What is the problem of method?

6 What are Thorndike's laws of learning? What help do these laws give in solving the problem of method?

7 What basis for understanding the function of aim or purpose is laid in Woodworth's analysis (S. Q. No. 53a, b)?

8. What is the psychology of purposeful learning? What other functions does the purpose perform in connection?

9. Do you see any connection of Q. 8 with Dewey's discussion of interest and of the relation of effort to interest? (*Interest and Effort*, pp. 14 *f.*, 43 *f.*, 46 *ff.*)

10. How fully do the foregoing considerations solve the problem of method?

BIBLIOGRAPHY

Source Quotations: 238; 86; 369; 142, 350; 244*, 343, 112, 284, 396.
Kilpatrick, *Project Method*.
Thorndike, *Educational Psychology*, Vol. II, Chaps. 1–4. (See also Table of Contents.) (*Briefer Course*, pp. 6 *ff.*, 50 *ff.*)
Dewey, *Democracy and Education*, Chaps. 12, 13, pp. 163 *ff.*, 256 *ff.*, 395 *ff.* (See also Table of Contents.)
Journal of Educational Method, 1:14–19, 54–59, 95–102, 144–150, 312–318, 367–374.
Monroe, *Cyclopedia of Education:* Learning, Method.
Strayer and Norsworthy, *How to Teach*, Chaps. 2, 4. (See also Table of Contents.)
Strayer, *The Teaching Process*, Chaps. 2, 3. (See also Table of Contents.)
Earhart, *Types of Teaching*, Chaps. 2, 3, 4. (See Table of Contents.)
Miller, *Education for the Needs of Life*, Chap. 5.
Bagley, *Educative Process*, Part VI.

Colvin, *The Learning Process*, Chaps. 1–4. (See Table of Contents.)
Woodworth, *Dynamic Psychology*, p. 36*f*.
Charters, *Methods of Teaching*, beginning with Chap. 13. (See Table
of Contents.)

26. CURRICULUM MAKING

1. Define generally the meaning of curriculum. What is the relation of the curriculum to subject matter? To educational outcomes? To educational aims? To method? To the philosophy of life?

2. What are the more important advantages and disadvantages that attend a curriculum prescribed in advance and from above?

3. What is meant by "deferred values"? What are the advantages and disadvantages of including such in a curriculum?

4. What practical value can come from listing educational aims? What advantage attaches here to the more specific? To the more general? What considerations forbid too long a list? Too short a list? Might hierarchical groupings of coördinate and mutually exclusive aims be useful?

5. Considering Q. 4, what suggestions can you make for forming a useful list of educational aims? Give illustrations of your idea.

6. What is meant by "minimum essentials"? What validity attaches to the conception?

7. What "ultimate" factors or aspects enter into the comparative valuation of specific educational outcomes? (Search for at least four mutually exclusive bases of comparison.)

8. What bearing on the curriculum has the accepted theory as to formal discipline?

9. Who should make the curriculum? When? How?

BIBLIOGRAPHY

Dewey, *Educational Situation*, pp. 27–34.
Thorndike, *Education*, pp. 127–130, Chaps. 2, 3, 7.
Dewey, *Democracy and Education*, Chaps. 8, 9, 18.
U. S. Bureau of Education Bulletin, 1918, No. 35, "Cardinal Principles of Secondary Education."
Inglis, *Principles of Secondary Education*, Chap. 10.
Bagley, *Educative Process*, Chaps. 3, 15; pp. 117 *ff.*
Monroe, *Cyclopedia of Education:* End in Education; Values, Educational.
Bagley, *Educational Values*, Chaps. 7–14.
Bobbitt, *The Curriculum*, Chap. 6.
Bonser, *Elementary School Curriculum*, Chaps. 2, 3.
Hanus, *Educational Aims and Educational Values*, Chaps. 1, 4, 5.
National Society for the Study of Education, 17th Year book, Part I, Section I.
Ruediger, *Principles of Education*, Chaps. 3, 4, 5, 7, 8.
Betts, *Social Principles of Education*, Chap. 3, pp. 101 *ff.*, 243 *ff.*

Spencer, *Education*, Chap. 1.
Sleight, *Educational Values and Methods*, Chaps. 6, 8, 9.
Butler, *Meaning of Education* (revised edition), pp. 22 *ff*., 103 *ff*.,
    Chap. 6.
O'Shea, *Education as Adjustment*, Chap. 4.

27. THE PROBLEM OF METHOD II

1. Give illustrations of the several types of "projects" (purposed activities or experiences) mentioned in S. Q. No. 408. What other classifications might be helpful?

2. If you had an additional step to propose to the analysis made of the first type (*Project Method*, p. 17), what would it be? What relations are there among the several steps of the analysis?

3. What is the "project" method? How is it related to the "problem" method? What disputes as to terminology belong here?

4. How does the conception of project teaching fit with our discussion of "Education its own end"?

5. To what extent might we expect to secure by the "project" method the minimum essentials of our present curriculum? Of a proper curriculum?

6. If this use of purposeful activity were adopted what changes would ensue as regards:
    a. The continued use of separate studies?
    b. The printed course of study?
    c. The daily program?
    d. The teacher's function?
    e. Grading and promotion?

7. What considerations chiefly favor the use of purposeful activity in the school room? What are the chief difficulties? What is at present feasible?

BIBLIOGRAPHY

Source Quotations: 408*; 247*; 149*, 112, 238, 244*.
Kilpatrick, *Project Method*.
Dewey, *Democracy and Education*, Chap. 8.
Dewey, *Educational Situation*, Part I.
Teachers College Record, 22:283–321.
Branom, *Project Method in Education* (see Index).
Bonser, *Elementary School Curriculum*, Chaps. 6, 7.
Stevenson, *Project Method of Teaching* (see Index).
School Science and Mathematics, 19:50–62 (Stevenson).
Monroe, *Cyclopedia of Education:* Activity, Method, Problem (Dewey).
Francis Parker School Studies in Education, 6:5–46 (Hall, "Individual Project Method").
Parker, *General Methods of Teaching in Elementary Schools*, Chap. 12.
Lull and Wilson, *Redirection of High School Instruction*, Chap. 4.
Teaching, Vol. 5, No. 1, "The Project Method of Instruction."
Elementary School Journal, 20:137–145 (Minor); 21:16–25, 98–111, 174–188, 257–272 (Parker); 112–116 (Horn).

Wilson, H. B. and Wilson, G. M., *Motivation of School Work* (see Index).

Lull, *Project Method of Learning* (see Index).

Cook, *The Play Way* (see Index).

Teachers College Record, 20: 99-106 (Kilpatrick); 21: 139-149 (Courtis).

Journal of Education, 92: 378-79 (Lull and Finch, "Problem-Project Method").

School and Home Education, 38: 209-215 (Stevenson, "Problems and Projects").

English Journal, 7: 599-603 (Hosic, "Outline of Problem-Project Method").

School and Society, 4: 419-423 (Snedden, "The Project as a Teaching Unit").

Educational Administration and Supervision, 5: 357-63 (Minor, "Supervision of Project Teaching").

28. VARIETY AND PROPORTION OF INTERESTS

1. What if any place have we allowed for a variety of interests in the curriculum?

2. Do all people feel the same interests? In the same relative degree? Is any difference here present due to nature or to nurture or to present available opportunity?

3. Is the social bearing of the several interests a matter of indifference?

4. Is it possible to substitute for any one native interest an equivalent combination of the remaining interests? Always? Never?

5. Does any combination of other interests ever seek to suppress or thwart any specific native interest or interests? Would such be wise? Never? Ever? How?

6. What striking combinations of interests thwartive of other interests has history to show as national or social ideals? What judgments has posterity passed upon these several instances?

7. Do we have among us at present any vocations that tend toward analogous thwartings? What is the social judgment?

8. Can any individual avoid continual choices that amount to at least temporary suppression? On what principle if any does one so choose? Is this proper?

9. What if any relationships exist between any of the foregoing and "activity leading to further activity"?

10. What if any bearing has Spencer's comparative values? What of B. Russell's insistence on impulsive activity (*Why Men Fight*, pp. 7 *f.*, 118 *f.*)?

11. What if any lessons do you draw from the foregoing for curriculum making? For life?

BIBLIOGRAPHY

Source Quotations: 22:284, 395:396; 293*, 376*, 308, 75: 7, 8, 113.
Russell, *Why Men Fight*, pp. 7–23, 31–38, 118–126.
Thorndike, *Educational Psychology*, Vol. I, pp. 17, 270 *f.*; Vol. III, Chaps. 3, 13.
Thorndike, *Education*, Chap. 3.
Marot, *Creative Impulse in Industry*, Introduction and Chap. 1.
Woodworth, *Dynamic Psychology*, pp. 174–176.
Charters, *Teaching the Common Branches*, Chap. 16.
Betts, *Social Principles of Education*, pp. 202–203.
Atlantic Monthly, 124:273–282 (Mansbridge, "The Universities and Labor").

29. ORGANIZATION

1. What practical interrelations have aim, organization, elements (data), process?

2. Is organization in the educative process an affair for the child or for the teacher? What should be the purpose of each?

3. What if any relation have organization and method? Would different theories of method mean different organizations? For the child or for the teacher?

4. What differences are indicated by the terms "logical organization" and "psychological organization"? Are these the same for all stages of growth?

5. What is meant by "psychologizing subject matter"? Wherein should the point of view of the teacher of science differ from that of the scientist?

6. What is a concept? What is it for? How is it formed? Has Q. 4 any bearing here?

7. What if any organization does the child make in the execution of a project? To what degree is project work consistent with systematic organization of subject-matter? How?

8. In what sense is organization an educational aim? How should it be sought?

9. What if any suggestion here for text-book making?

BIBLIOGRAPHY

Source Quotations: 159, 210, 213*, 229.
McMurry, *How to Study* (see Index).
Journal of Educational Method, 1: 276–283.
Dewey, *Child and Curriculum,* pp. 25–30; *School and Child,* pp. 33–42.
Dewey, *How We Think,* pp. 56–63.
McMurry, *Elementary School Standards* (see Index).
Betts, *Classroom Methods and Management,* Chap. 8.
Breese, *Psychology,* Chap. 13.
James, *Psychology, Brief Course,* Chap. 14.

30. MORAL EDUCATION

1. Does Thorndike's (secular) psychology suffice for the discussion of this topic? If not, what else is needed?

2. Having in mind character building, can you propose one or more helpful analyses of moral character? (Compare Dewey, *Moral Principles*, p. 49 *f.*, S. Q. No. 218). What is the genetic psychology correlative of each of your analyses? What the correlative school procedure?

3. What do you think of the use of stories or pictures for character building? Is the good effect of a good story as great as the bad effect of a bad story? If yes, how so? If no, why not?

4. What is the psychology of coercion? One "set" or more? Any satisfaction? Any learning? Any new interest possible?

5. In the development of moral character.
    a. What is the effect of a difficulty? Always? What is the effect of interest?
    b. What functions has punishment?
    c. How do social approval and disapproval act?
    d. What effect have diversities of codes and judgments?

6. How do you conceive the relatively automatic and the deliberate to be united in a moral character? What corollary here for education? What about military discipline?

7. What do you think of "direct" moral instruction?

8. Is it possible to prepare against the day of temptation? And not rely on formal discipline?

9. In the light of all the foregoing what practical plan for moral character education do you advocate?

BIBLIOGRAPHY

Source Quotations: 218*, 398*, 16* (a, b, d), 369, 351, 352, 64; 350*, 94*, 114*, 170, 187, 399; 16*c, 158*, 323; 313*, 330*, 251, 335, 134, 144, 252; 195, 196; 16* (e, f), 394.
Dewey, *Moral Principles in Education.*
James, *Talks to Teachers*, Chaps. 4, 8, 15.
Kilpatrick, *Project Method.*
Journal of Educational Method, 1:182–189, 233–239, 415–421.
Thorndike, *Educational Psychology*, Vol. II, p. 419.
Religious Education, 6:485–492 (Coe, "Virtue and the Virtues").
Religious Education, 14:123–147 (Kilpatrick and Coe, "Education of Adolescents for Democracy").
Monroe, *Cyclopedia of Education:* Moral Character.
James, *Psychology*, Vol. I, Chaps. 4, 10; Vol. II, Chap. 26.

Thorndike, *Education* (see Index).
MacDougall, *Social Psychology*, Chaps. 7, 8.
Bagley, *School Discipline* (see Index).
MacCunn, *The Making of Character.*

SUGGESTED TOPICS FOR TERM PAPERS*

1. Experience is the ultimate universe of discourse.
2. Fatalism and determinism in relation to endeavor.
3. Deterministic psychology and ethics.
4. The elements constitutive of society—a comparative study of different statements.
5. Education as a solution of the (so-called) conflict between society and the individual.
6. Education as a unifying element in America.
7. Social solidarity as an educational objective.
8. The psychological meaning of "internal" vs. "external" choices.
9. The application of Kant's dictum (S. Q. No. 2) to prevailing social practices.
10. Differing historic conceptions of freedom.
11. Enlightened selfishness as a basis of ethics.
12. The educational philosophy and correlative educational scheme of Plato (or Aristotle, St. Jerome, Luther, Calvin, Wesley, Voltaire, Napoleon, Jefferson, Horace Mann, or Tolstoi).
13. The psychological meaning of self and its genesis.
14. The socialization of the country woman (or girl or boy or man).
15. The principal demands of present American life upon American education.
16. Distinctive American characteristics as shown by foreign criticism.
17. Foreign criticism of American education.
18. Is democracy properly styled "the cult of the incompetent"?
19. Wherein is America a democracy?
20. Industrial democracy and education.
21. Historic democratic tendencies in American education.
22. Historic changes in American education toward democracy or away from it.
23. A detailed contrast of any two historic schemes of education from the point of view of democracy.
24. The application of Dewey's criterion (*Democracy and Education*, pp. 95 *f.*) to some of our prevailing social institutions.
25. Democratic and non-democratic elements in American education (or in English or French 1790–1914 or Prussian 1760–1914 or modern Japanese education).
26. Present dangers to democracy in America.

*These are suggestive of possible topics. As given they are not intended to be mutual exclusives.

27. The problem of democracy in relation to the junior high school.
28. Desirable changes in American education so as to bring greater equality of educational opportunities.
29. Democratic respect for the expert.
30. Varying respect for personality shown in different historic educational schemes.
31. War essentially anti-democratic.
32. War a proper and permanent agency of civilization.
33. A study of the factors affecting pronouncedly the socialization of any given community.
34. The meaning of progress (or of social progress).
35. Is progress a fact of history?
36. What brings progress?
37. Historic evidences of fluctuation in progress.
38. To what extent if at all is social stability dependent upon indoctrination and the like?
39. Factors that now threaten social stability in this (or any other) country.
40. The mobilization (organization) of our country's thinking to social ends.
41. The effort to Prussianize North Slesvig (or Poland or Alsace-Lorraine).
42. The philosophy of American education in the Philippines (or in Porto Rico or Hawaii or with the Alaskan Eskimos).
43. The demand for excitement and its proper expression.
44. Genesis of the 1915–16 demand for "preparedness."
45. The genesis of military patriotism.
46. The university and public opinion in Germany (prior to 1914).
47. The university as a factor in forming public opinion in America.
48. The critical attitude of American public opinion towards the university.
49. The American high school in relation to the direction of American public opinion.
50. Voluntary associations in relation to the formation of public opinion.
51. How can the schools below college grade raise the standards of American political life?
52. Methods and aims of propagandism in the United States (or in any other country).
53. What can the schools do as regards dangers from the press or from moving pictures.
54. The philosophy of American vocational education.
55. Freedom of speech as a social factor.
56. Freedom of speech in American life.
57. Academic freedom.

58. Freedom of teaching in schools lower than university grade.
59. Democracy, public opinion, and academic freedom.
60. A historic study of infringement upon freedom of speech (or of teaching) at any period in any country.
61. The holding of radical political views a bar to teaching in the public secondary school. (Take any position you wish.)
62. Tenure of office in relation to academic freedom and educational efficiency.
63. Limitations upon academic freedom in the university (or in the arts college or in the public school).
64. Academic freedom in relation to social progress.
65. Limitations upon teaching in state schools.
66. What attitude shall the public school take toward highly controversial questions?
67. The proper government of universities.
68. The proper function of trustees in the management of a university.
69. Should teachers join the labor union movement?
70. Organized labor and public education.
71. The educational programs of organized labor.
72. Limitations upon government control of education.
73. The problem of "centralization" in democratic school administration.
74. The demands of democracy on school administration.
75. The demands of democracy on school supervision.
76. Mutual relationships of superintendent, supervisor and teacher in consideration of the demands of efficiency and of democracy.
77. Administrative uniformity as regards curriculum in a system of schools.
78. The right and propriety of taxing for public education those who prefer non-public schools.
79. Division of public school funds among semi-public and non-public school systems.
80. Social principles involved in raising and apportioning public school funds.
81. A democratic education for varying native abilities.
82. Shall the government make the curriculum?
83. Limitations upon governmental support of education.
84. Compulsory school attendance: its justification and limitations.
85. An examination of the case against democratic control of education.
86. The *laissez faire* attitude toward state support and control of education.
87. A democratic program for moral education.
88. The relation between religious and general education.
89. Place of parochial school systems in a democracy.

90. Place of private schools in a democracy.
91. State supervision of non-public schools.
92. In what sense should immigrants be assimilated and why?
93. The agencies of assimilation at work in America.
94. Duty of America to the adult immigrant.
95. Duty of the school in relation to "Americanization."
96. Americanization: meaning of, necessity for, limitations upon.
97. Special educational needs of the immigrant child.
98. The maintenance in America of the immigrant's historic cultural connections.
99. The proper attitude towards the exclusive use of the English language in our schools, in our newspapers, among our people, in our dependencies.
100. The problem of religious education.
101. The education of backward peoples.
102. Missionary education.
103. Feminization of the teaching profession.
104. The philosophy of higher education of women is this (or any other) country. A historic study.
105. The education of women.
106. Determination of the proper distribution of the educative function among the principal educative institutions.
107. Historic variation in the distribution of the education function.
108. A code of professional ethics for educators.
109. The most serviceable definitions of education.
110. "Education has no end beyond itself."
111. A study of the terms curriculum, subject-matter, and method.
112. Training and education.
113. A democratic program for vocational education.
114. How method in education varies with different systems of philosophy.
115. Varying historic types of educational method.
116. The problem of school room method in a democracy.
117. A restatement of Dewey's doctrine of interest in terms of Thorndike's laws of learning.
118. A comparison of method here and abroad.
119. Historical study of the American attitude towards method.
120. The problem of method in ancient classical education.
121. The psychology of compulsion and its educational corollaries.
122. Military training in the public school.
123. The transfer value of military training.
124. The educational theory of punishments.
125. "Logical" *vs.* "psychological" organization with implications for method.
126. The practical school room use of the conception of "concomitants."

127. Play in education.
128. The social bearing of play activities.
129. The problem of method in the college and university.
130. The proper place of coercion.
131. The administration of the "project method."
132. The course of study on the "project" basis.
133. Changes in school management demanded by the "project method."
134. Geography teaching according to the "project method."
135. History teaching according to the "project method."
136. Present actual use of the "project method" in school and out.
137. The limitations of the "project method."
138. "Deferred values."
139. Influence of the doctrine of interest on the curriculum.
140. Desirable changes in the elementary curriculum.
141. Minimum essentials critically considered.
142. Doctrines of recapitulation in relation to curriculum making.
143. Criteria for judging physical education.
144. What changes are necessary to bring the elementary and secondary curriculum into accord with the best current doctrine of transfer training?
145. The educational bearings of the Regents' (or other centralized external) examination system.
146. To what extent should we retain distinct studies below the senior high school?
147. Needed changes in the high school curriculum.
148. The content of a "culture" course in junior high school mathematics based on the minimum essentials procedure.
149. The reorganization and reconstitution of high school Latin.
150. The determination of the proper content of arithmetic (or of geography or history or any other school subject).
151. The college curriculum.
152. A college curriculum for a dynamic society.
153. The text-book in arithmetic as the correlative of educational method—a historical study (or the same for geography or grammar or history).
154. The text-book in religion as the correlative of educational method —a historical study.
155. Criteria for judging text-books in geography (or for any other school subject.
156. Patriotism: what it means; how it should be taught.
157. The teaching of patriotism in the secondary school.
158. The teaching of patriotism in the elementary school.
159. Education in civic patriotism.
160. Education for citizenship.